W9-CQF-300

CONTENTS

THE WILL TO SURVIVE

Gail Blasser Riley
with Margo Sorenson

STECK-VAUGHN
ELEMENTARY · SECONDARY · ADULT · LIBRARY

A Harcourt Company

www.steck-vaughn.com

Photography: Cover ©Dave Martin AP/Wide World Photos; p.iv ©Julie Habel/CORBIS; p.6 ©Reuters NewMedia Inc./ CORBIS; pp.10–11, 13 ©AP/Wide World Photos; p.19 ©Bettmann/CORBIS; pp.30, 34 ©AP/Wide World Photos; p.37 ©Courtesy NOAA.

Additional photography by CORBIS and Cartesia.

Art: p.3 Gary Antonetti.

CHAPTER 1

LOST IN THE SNOW

The wind roared outside the tiny cave. Coyotes howled. Inside the cave Jennifer Stolpa pulled her baby closer.

Outside lay **endless** drifts of snow. Inside, Jennifer struggled to stay alive. She melted snow in her mouth for water. It had been days since her last meal.

Jennifer's husband, Jim, had left two days ago. He went to find help. Was he still alive?

The struggle had begun nine days earlier for Jim, Jennifer, and their baby, Clayton. They'd left their home in Paso Robles, California, to go to Idaho. They would have to travel 800 miles to get to the funeral of Jim's grandmother. It was late December 1992, and winter was in full force.

◀ *Blizzards make driving difficult and dangerous.*

The Stolpas had planned to drive their truck across Nevada on Interstate 80, but a blizzard had covered the highway with snow. The highway was closed. Jim and Jennifer decided to travel across smaller roads. They thought those roads would not be closed.

They drove through the tiny town of Vya, Nevada. Then they **ventured** down County Road 8A. It was a small dirt road that headed toward State Route 140. No other cars were on that road. Snow covered the road and continued to fall. Finally the Stolpas' truck got stuck. They could go no farther.

Jennifer and Jim decided to wait, hoping a **rescuer** might find them. They hadn't packed much food, though. They only had some cookies, cake, chips, and **vitamins**.

Days went by. Snow kept falling. During that time the Stolpas turned on the engine for short times to run the truck's heater. They knew their gas wouldn't last **indefinitely**. Their food was almost gone, too.

The trip from Paso Robles to Pocatello ▶
was cut short by heavy snows.

After four days, Jim and Jennifer knew they would have to search for help, or they would not survive. They left a note on the truck to tell any **potential** rescuers where they were headed.

The two put on almost every piece of clothing they had packed. They put garbage bags between layers of socks. Then they snuggled Clayton inside two sleeping bags and a clothing bag.

Jim hooked the clothing bag to his belt to make a sled for the baby. The Stolpas walked through snow all day and night in search of Route 140. They never found it.

Trudging through many feet of snow in fierce wind was hard work. After going about 20 miles, Jennifer knew she couldn't walk any farther. Jim would have to go on alone.

They found a tiny cave. It was so small that Jennifer and Clayton could barely fit inside. Jennifer could not even sit up. At least she and Clayton would be out of the snow.

Jim put the clothing bag over the cave's entrance to block the harsh winds. He hung a blue **sweatshirt** on a nearby bush for a flag. He promised Jennifer that he'd get help within three days. Then he set off across the snow.

Jim struggled through the snow for mile after mile. Inside his tennis shoes, ice caked over his feet. Flakes of blowing ice and snow bit at his face. His stomach groaned with hunger **pangs**. Jim grew weaker, but he kept going. His wife and son depended on him.

Jim kept walking for two days, resting as briefly as possible. Finally he saw a truck driving through the snow. He shouted and waved until the driver saw him.

The driver drove Jim to Vya, where Jim gave rescue workers directions to find Jennifer and Clayton. Hours went by as the rescuers struggled to find their way in the snow.

At last someone spotted the blue sweatshirt. Jennifer and Clayton were weak, but they were still alive. The Stolpa family had made it.

Blizzard!

The Stolpas' problems started because of a blizzard. When does a **snowstorm** turn into a blizzard? The wind speed must be at least 35 miles per hour. The storm must last at least three hours in a single place. Temperatures must be very low—usually lower than twenty degrees Fahrenheit. Finally, **visibility** must be low. In a blizzard the wind blows so much snow that people can't see very far in front of them. It's easy to lose your way if you are trying to walk or drive through a blizzard. ⚡

Two men struggle to free a car that is stuck in snow.

CHAPTER 2

THE EARTH SHAKES APART

People in India were excited as they prepared to celebrate Republic Day on January 26, 2001. That day was a national holiday. All over India people joined parades and other **celebrations**. They had no idea that an earthquake was about to rock western India.

In Gandhidham joy turned to fear and panic as the ground suddenly began to shake and break apart. People screamed and dashed in every direction. The sounds of cracking and **explosions** rang through the town. Buildings shook wildly and fell to pieces. Metal and **concrete** shot into the air and then raced like rockets to the ground.

The shaking lasted for about a minute. When it ended, piles of rubble lay where stores, apartments, and homes had stood just a moment before. Clouds of dust filled the air. People cried out for help.

Many thousands of people lost their lives during the earthquake. The Chelappan family was lucky, though.

On that morning in Gandhidham, Chitra Chelappan was in her kitchen with her husband, Silveira, and their six-year-old daughter, Gita. The morning seemed like many others.

Suddenly the ground began to shake. Walls cracked and moved, then fell apart. The house fell in. When the earthquake stopped, the Chelappans found safety in a small, sheltered space in the mess. They could not escape to the outside. Their home had become a prison of rubble. For five days the Chelappans could do nothing but wait for help.

The earthquake hit ▶
Gandhidham hard.

How did the family survive? In their tiny space they found tomatoes and a bottle of water. These items and patience kept the family alive for five long days. All were alive when the rescuers pulled them from the ruins of their home.

Earthquake!

Why do earthquakes happen? Earth's surface, or **crust**, is made up of large masses of rock. These masses are called **plates**. The plates are moving all the time.

The places where these plates meet one another are called **faults**. The plates move along the faults, usually very slowly.

An earthquake occurs upon the sudden movement of two plates. **Vibrations** ripple out through the surrounding rock and land. Watch what happens when you drop a stone into a tub of water. You can get a good idea of how an earthquake's vibrations travel.

The strength, or **magnitude**, of an earthquake is measured on the Richter scale. Numbers on the scale go from 1 to 10 or higher. They describe the amount of energy given off by the earthquake. Each number represents a magnitude ten times stronger than the number before it.

If an earthquake is higher than 6 on the Richter scale, it can cause a great deal of damage. The 2001 Republic Day earthquake measured 7.7. Luckily for the Chelappans, this serious earthquake did not destroy the small, sheltered space in their kitchen.

The Republic Day earthquake caused this building to fall.

CHAPTER 3

GIANT WALLS OF WATER

On July 17, 1998, the sun set after a quiet day in Papua New Guinea. Small villages dotted the beaches and jungles along the northern coast. Villagers finished fishing or tending their gardens. Some returned to their small, wooden huts. Others walked along the beach, enjoying the calm night. Some sat and visited with friends.

Meanwhile, 12 miles away, a powerful earthquake ripped the sea floor apart, far below the Pacific Ocean. As it did so, it caused great movements of water. Energy from the movements spread out across the ocean. Within moments the first of three giant waves approached the shore of Papua New Guinea. Villagers heard a loud roar from the ocean. It was all that warned them of the first **tsunami** rushing toward them.

An earthquake caused the tsunamis ▶
that leveled this village.

The wave crashed onto the shore, sweeping through the villages. The second wave came minutes later. It was the tallest wave, about thirty feet high. Then the last wave struck. Some people and homes were carried far into the jungle. Others floated out into the ocean. Thousands of people drowned in the rushing waters. Others died as they slammed into the jungle trees or were struck by floating **debris**. Whole villages were washed away.

Those who lived had amazing stories to tell. When the tsunamis hit, Ita Atopi was with her one-month-old twins, Alphonse and Jenny.

Instead of fighting the waves, Atopi rode them. She tied her babies to her body. She stayed calm and watched for a way to help herself and her children. When a coconut tree floated by, Atopi grabbed it. She pulled herself onto it. Atopi and her babies lived through the disaster.

Blandien Sapien was cooking dinner in her hut when the giant waves hit Papua New Guinea. In an instant she found herself at the top of a coconut tree with her two-week-old baby.

Sapien held her baby and gripped tightly onto the tree until the water level dropped. Then she reached out to grab a floating branch. She and her baby floated away.

Sapien grew weaker and weaker as she struggled against the waves. She handed her baby to another person floating nearby. When Sapien gained enough strength, she swam to shore. Later, she found her baby, who was safe and well.

Since that terrible night, many of the remaining villagers have moved to the mountains of Papua New Guinea. They say that they will never feel safe near the beach again.

Tsunami!

The tsunami in Papua New Guinea was caused by an earthquake under the ocean. However, an earthquake is not the only cause of tsunamis. Another cause is the **eruption** of underwater volcanoes.

These events can disturb water deep in the ocean. Energy spreads out through the water, making waves. Far out at sea, the waves are low, so ships might not even notice the changes in the water. Tsunamis are powerful, though. Their waves can travel faster than jet airplanes.

Tsunami waves get higher the farther they travel. Near shore, the water slows down as it is pulled into a chain of giant waves. These waves can be taller than 150 feet.

Some people call a tsunami a **tidal** wave, but it is not one. Tides are changes in the height of the ocean. They are caused by the pull of the moon or sun, so they go through a regular **cycle** of rising and falling every day. Tides cannot produce the giant tsunamis.

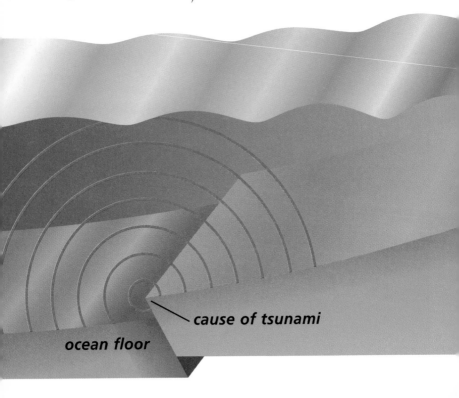

cause of tsunami

ocean floor

Many countries are trying to find ways to warn people when tsunamis are approaching. If people have a warning, they can get to higher ground. Tsunamis travel quickly, so there are only a few minutes to act. These few minutes can mean the difference between life and death.

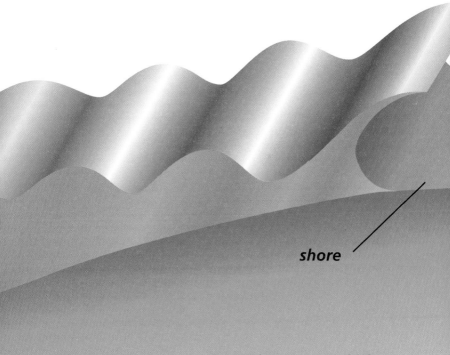

shore

Tsunami waves grow higher as they approach the shore.

CHAPTER 4

RAGING FIRES

It was early September 2001 in the Tahoe National Forest in California. A fire was raging across the land. Lack of summer rain had made the forest very dry, so when the fire began, it spread quickly. It had already burned almost 14,000 acres. However, the fire seemed as if it were under control.

On September 8, 2001, Fire Chief Geoff Wilford **supervised** the crews fighting the fire. He heard a voice calling him on his radio. The branch director asked him to help check the **fire line** near the highway. The crews had changed the fire line during the night. Chief Wilford agreed to help check it and headed there in his truck.

A crew cuts a fire line to stop a ▶ forest fire from spreading.

The fire line was a line where the **hotshot crews** had cleared the forest. Hotshot crews are **firefighters** that are trained to build fire lines. They chopped trees and bushes down to the bare dirt. If there was nothing to burn, the fire could not spread. The crews cut away all the lower branches of some trees. This would make it harder for the fire to find fuel. From above, helicopters dropped water on the fire line.

The crews also had been setting **backfires** at the fire line. These smaller fires burn up all the remaining wood and other fuel in the area. The main fire will stop when it meets the backfires.

At first, the backfires were working. The main fire was **contained** along the fire line. Chief Wilford walked along the line. As he did so, he studied the smoke. Suddenly he tightened his jaw. The wind was changing. Soon it would be blowing the fire and backfires right at the crews.

Chief Wilford jumped in his truck. He drove to a safe spot near the fire line. As he opened the truck door to get out, a wall of orange and yellow flames was all he could see. Quickly, Chief Wilford called the hotshot crews on his radio.

Dry weather makes fires hard to control.

The sky turned dark as smoke blocked out the sun. Pieces of burning twigs and pine needles floated through the air. They blew over the fire line and across the highway. They landed in the green area of the forest. There they started hundreds of small fires. The new fires were out of control! If the crews didn't act fast, the fire would spread quickly across the rest of the forest.

Soon fire engines began rolling in. Their headlights shined through the dark air. Their sirens wailed. High above, helicopter blades chopped the air.

The main fire roared closer. It sounded like jet airplanes taking off. The heat was fierce. The wind only made it worse. Burning twigs hissed through the air.

Hotshot crews hopped out of their trucks. They grabbed their shovels, axes, and rakes. They also took chain saws and began clearing a new fire line.

A helicopter picks up water from a river to drop on a fire.

Chief Wilford stood on top of the cab of his pickup, guiding the fire engines to the burning spots. Firefighters started laying out hoses. Others went into the forest. Helicopters brought hundreds of gallons of water.

While many firefighters worked to control the main fire, the hotshot crews cut a new fire line. In time they circled the new fires that had begun on the other side of the road. The team began winning the battle.

The winds died down. The fire line was in place. The main fire couldn't spread anymore. Though the fire wouldn't be completely controlled until September 13, the hotshot crews and other firefighters had contained it once again. They would continue working until all of the fires were out.

Fire!

All fires need three things in order to burn—fuel, heat, and oxygen.

Fuel is what burns in a fire. Fuel can be underground, at the surface, or above the ground. How fast the fuel burns depends on what size it is, how wet or dry it is, and where it is located. Fuel can be logs, paper, leaves, coal, buildings, or other things. Also, some liquids, such as gasoline, can be very **flammable**. Fuels such as wood and paper burn faster if they are dry. Heat starts the fire. A spark from a campfire, tobacco products, or a lightning strike can easily start a fire in the wilderness. If there is a lot of fuel nearby, the fire can spread rapidly.

Oxygen is a gas in the air. Fire needs this gas in order to keep burning. Some small fires can be put out by covering them. Doing this keeps air out so the fire can't burn.

Weather affects fires. Wind, temperature, and **humidity** all make a difference. Wind feeds the fire with oxygen. It also blows sparks and bits of burning fuel that spread the fire. A fire spreads more slowly in cooler temperatures. Humidity, or water in the air, is also important. It makes fuel moist, causing it to burn more slowly.

Fires can be dangerous for people and animals, but in some ways they are good for nature. Some forests need fire to stay healthy and to keep growing. Certain seeds only open when burned by a fire. Without fire, new plants can't grow from these seeds. Other plants grow stronger after a forest fire because tall trees no longer block the sun.

CHAPTER 5

STORM FROM THE SEA

On August 17, 1992, a **tropical storm** formed over the Atlantic Ocean. As it moved west over the warm ocean waters, its winds grew stronger. By August 22, the storm had become a hurricane, named Andrew. It moved toward South Florida.

People heard the news on televisions and radios. Many businesses and schools in South Florida closed. People began to flee the area. Long lines of cars headed away from South Florida. In airports people begged for open seats on flights. People could already feel the winds growing stronger as the hurricane moved closer.

Some people decided to stay in their homes. They did what they could to prepare for the hurricane. They nailed boards over their windows.

Winds whirl around a calm center.

They took inside anything that could be picked up and thrown by the storm's raging winds. They gathered bottled water, food, and radios.

Late in the day on August 22, the skies began to grow dark. Winds sent papers, dirt, and small branches flying. Waves grew taller. Police officers walked up and down the beach telling people to **evacuate** their beach homes immediately.

As night fell, the roads became empty. It was too late to try to drive away from the storm. Many thousands of people filled shelters. They waited for Hurricane Andrew to arrive.

The next morning, Hurricane Andrew was only 12 miles away. The fast winds spun the dark storm clouds around and around over the ocean. Heavy rain fell. As the day passed, the people who stayed in South Florida continued to wait and to prepare for the storm.

Early the next morning, Hurricane Andrew reached land. Its howling winds blew as fast as 150 miles per hour. The storm ripped entire houses from their foundations and broke them into thousands of pieces.

The windows shattered in a school shelter. Water flooded into classrooms and the auditorium. The lunchroom floor disappeared underwater.

At the Miami Metro Zoo, winds tossed trailers and destroyed roofs. Pieces of metal sailed through the air and ripped apart fences. Hard rain smacked at the animals. Many of them escaped from their cages. Hundreds of birds flew out into the storm. A herd of **antelope** galloped into the raging wind and rain. Tortoises, each weighing more than 500 pounds, escaped from their zoo homes.

Apes, lions, tigers, and bears listened to the storm slamming against their night houses. The steel and concrete surrounding them kept them safe.

In Kendall, Florida, near Miami, a husband and wife huddled in their small downstairs bathroom as the hurricane tore at their house. They could hear tiles ripping away from their roof. The bathroom ceiling began to bend. Windows throughout the house shattered. The wind pushed against the bathroom door all night long.

By 7:30 A.M., the winds slowed. The couple stepped cautiously out of their bathroom. They discovered that all the rooms in their home, except the tiny bathroom and a closet, had been destroyed. In fact, homes all over South Florida had been destroyed by Hurricane Andrew. The town of Homestead was leveled.

Hurricane Andrew damaged many communities in South Florida.

Hurricane Andrew cut a path of destruction across South Florida. Then it headed along the Gulf of Mexico, hitting Louisiana with its terrible power. Andrew caused about 26 billion dollars' worth of damage—more than any other natural disaster had ever caused. It would be many years before people would recover from the storm.

Hurricane!

A hurricane brews over warm ocean waters. As the sun heats the water, **water vapor** rises through the air. The hot, moist air rises.

When the warm, moist air rises and meets cool air, the air begins to spin. As the air spins faster and faster, a tropical storm forms. The storm becomes a hurricane when the winds reach 74 miles per hour. Rain, wind, and clouds form a wall around a calm center. This center is called the *eye* of the hurricane.

Some hurricanes, like Andrew, can reach speeds of more than 150 miles per hour. Hurricanes have more energy than any other storms on Earth.

At the beginning of each hurricane season, the World Meteorological Organization issues the list of names that will be given to hurricanes.

Most hurricane names are repeated every six years. If a hurricane causes great loss and damage, its name can be removed from the list. The name *Andrew* will never be used again.

Saffir-Simpson Hurricane Scale

CATEGORY	WINDS (miles per hour)	EFFECTS
1	74–95	Damage to mobile homes, shrubs, and trees
2	96–110	Some damage to roofs, doors, and windows; serious damage to plants, mobile homes, and docks
3	111–130	Damage to small homes; destruction of mobile homes
4	131–155	Major damage to lower floors and roofs of buildings near the shore; flooding of homes up to 6 miles from shore
5	greater than 155	Major damage to lower floors and roofs of all buildings within 500 yards of the shore; flooding of homes 5–10 miles from shore

CHAPTER 6

RISING WATERS

As the rain pounded in early June 2001, Al Amaral watched streams of water forming in the streets of Houston, Texas. The water was getting higher and higher. Amaral dashed to check on his business and his nine dogs. Before he knew it, the water had climbed inside his building, and it was still climbing. To escape the rising water, Amaral raced up onto the roof. Eight of his dogs followed him, but he wasn't able to find the ninth.

Nearby houses disappeared beneath a river of **floodwater.** The floodwater rose closer and closer to the roof of Amaral's building.

During the Houston flood, rafts and boats could go where cars could not.

For 36 hours, Amaral and his dogs sat on the roof. The rain pounded, and the river rose. Amaral had no food. Although there was water all around, he didn't have a drop to drink. He knew the dirty floodwater wasn't safe. It was filled with germs, floating balls of fire ants, and many other dangers.

Amaral also knew he couldn't be the only person in the Houston area caught in the flood. He knew he had to stay calm and wait for help.

Friends on the ground across from Amaral's business finally spotted him. In addition, a Houston television station showed him on his roof and called the U. S. Coast Guard to rescue the man. A TV news show asked that anyone nearby send help for Al Amaral and his dogs.

Some people heard the news and headed toward Amaral in a boat. The Coast Guard sent a helicopter. However, Amaral's friends made it across the water in a boat and rescued him and his dogs just before the other help arrived. People showed the same kind of help and kindness to others all over the city.

What caused this flood? Tropical Storm Allison had begun to build in the Gulf of Mexico just days before. It wasn't a strong storm, so people in Houston didn't expect it to give them much trouble. Allison surprised them. Rain began to fall on Wednesday and didn't stop for five days. **Rainfall**, which is usually measured in inches, was measured in feet.

Water rose quickly—more quickly than anyone had expected. Roads became rushing rivers. Water rose to the roofs of huge trucks. Drivers opened windows and scrambled to truck rooftops to wait for help. Television stations reported the news all day and night.

When hospitals flooded, patients had to be moved during the storm. One woman lost her life when she took an elevator to an underground parking lot to move her car to higher ground. The floodwater broke through the parking lot wall and rushed through the garage. Other people died when they were swept away by dangerous **flash floods.**

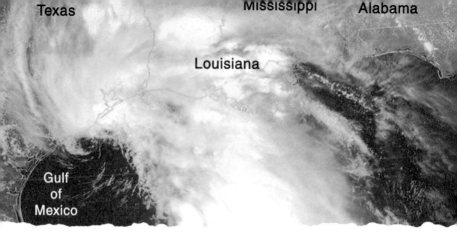

This picture shows Tropical Storm Allison in a view from space.

On Monday, the people in the Houston area woke up to clear, blue skies. As the water began to **recede**, people could see all the damage that Tropical Storm Allison had caused. Officials said the damage was about five billion dollars' worth.

Flood!

Usually when it rains, water soaks into the soil. When a flood occurs, it is often because of heavy rain. The soil can't hold all that extra water. Some of the water runs off and flows into rivers. With the added water, rivers spill over their banks. Water spreads across the land.

In cities, much of the soil has been covered with concrete or other materials, so water can't soak in. If there is a lot of rain, much of the water can't go into the ground. It starts to collect and can become a flood. This storm water can be joined by water from flooding rivers. That is what happened in Houston.

Floods also can happen when winter turns to spring in areas of heavy snow. Warm temperatures can melt the snow quickly. As the extra water runs into rivers, the rivers can flood their banks.

Flash floods are sudden movements of walls of water down a river or other area. In seconds, they can wash away cars and people. It is important never to walk or drive into areas that might be in danger of flash flooding during or after a storm. Even if the rain has stopped, there might be water rushing down rivers or dry creek beds from higher areas.

Disasters—A Natural Challenge

When many people think of nature, they think of quiet walks in a forest or along a shore. There's more to nature than that. Disasters like the ones you've just read about are also part of the natural world.

People cannot prevent hurricanes, earthquakes, or other disasters. When natural disasters strike, people struggle against nature. These disasters can be powerful and cause a lot of damage, but people have a strong will to survive. When you see news stories about natural disasters, you also will find stories about people like the Stolpas, the Chelappans, and others—stories of people who've survived. People can't always control or tame nature, but they will always fight to survive.

GLOSSARY

antelope (AN tuh lohp) *noun* Antelope are fast deer-like animals with horns.

backfires (BAK fyrz) *noun* Backfires are small fires used to burn away bushes and branches so that a main fire cannot find fuel.

celebrations (sehl uh BRAY shuhnz) *noun* Celebrations are fun activities for special times.

concrete (KAHN kreet) *noun* Concrete is a hard material used in building. It is made of sand, pebbles, water, and cement.

contained (kuhn TAYND) *adjective* A fire is contained if it cannot spread.

crust (KRUHST) *noun* The hard, rocky outer part of Earth is the crust.

cycle (SY kuhl) *noun* A cycle is a set of events that happen over and over again in the same order.

debris (duh BREE) *noun* Debris is all the broken pieces of wood, glass, and other materials that are left after something has been destroyed.

endless (EHND lihs) *adjective* Something that is endless goes on and on.

eruption (ee RUHP shuhn) *noun* An eruption is a burst of lava or ash from a volcano.

evacuate (ee VAK yoo ayt) *verb* To evacuate is to leave and seek safety.

explosions (ehk SPLOH zhuhnz) *noun* Explosions are sudden bursts with loud noises.

faults (FAWLTS) *noun* Faults are places where large masses of Earth's rocky layer meet.

firefighters (FYR fyt uhrz) *noun* Firefighters are people who put out fires.

fire line (FYR LYN) *noun* A fire line is a line of cleared land that has no fuel left for a fire to burn.

flammable (FLAM uh buhl) *adjective* Something that is flammable can burn easily.

flash floods (FLASH FLUHDZ) *noun* Flash floods are sudden rushes of water after a heavy rain.

floodwater (FLUHD wawt uhr) *noun* Floodwater is water that is flowing outside of a river or stream during a flood.

hotshot crews (HAHT shaht KROOZ) *noun* Hotshot crews are groups of people who are trained to clear areas and to keep a fire from spreading.

humidity (hyoo MIHD uh tee) *noun* Humidity is the amount of water in the air.

indefinitely (ihn DEHF uh niht lee) *adverb* Indefinitely means without a known end.

magnitude (MAG nuh tood) *noun* Magnitude is the amount of energy released during an earthquake.

pangs (PANGZ) *noun* Pangs are sudden feelings of pain.

plates (PLAYTS) *noun* Plates are large masses of rock on Earth. They move slowly over time. Earthquakes can occur where two plates move against each other.

potential (poh TEHN shuhl) *adjective* Potential means possible.

rainfall (RAYN fawl) *noun* Rainfall is the amount of rain that has fallen in an area during a period of time.

recede (rih SEED) *verb* To recede means to move back.

rescuer (REHS kyoo uhr) *noun* A rescuer is someone who helps save a person from danger.

snowstorm (SNOH stawrm) *noun* A snowstorm is a storm in which there is heavy snow and possibly strong winds.

supervised (SOO puhr vyzd) *verb* Supervised means watched over a project and the people who worked on it.

sweatshirt (SWEHT shurt) *noun* A sweatshirt is a heavy, loose, long-sleeved shirt.

tidal (TYD uhl) *adjective* Tidal means having to do with tides, the rising and falling of the surface of oceans from the pull of the sun or moon.

tropical storm (TRAHP ih kuhl STAWRM) *noun* A tropical storm is a storm that begins over warm oceans. Its winds blow 39–73 miles per hour. It can bring heavy rain.

tsunami (tsoo NAH mee) *noun* A tsunami is a giant wave, usually caused by a sudden earthquake under an ocean. Usually two or more tsunamis form in such an event.

ventured (VEHN chuhrd) *verb* Ventured means bravely headed into danger.

vibrations (vy BRAY shuhnz) *noun* Vibrations are slight movements back and forth.

visibility (vihz uh BIHL uh tee) *noun* Visibility is the ability to see across a distance in a certain light or in certain weather conditions.

vitamins (VYT uh mihnz) *noun* Vitamins are a type of medicine. People take vitamins to give their bodies things they need but might not get from their food.

water vapor (WAWT uhr VAY puhr) *noun* Water vapor is water in the form of a gas.

INDEX